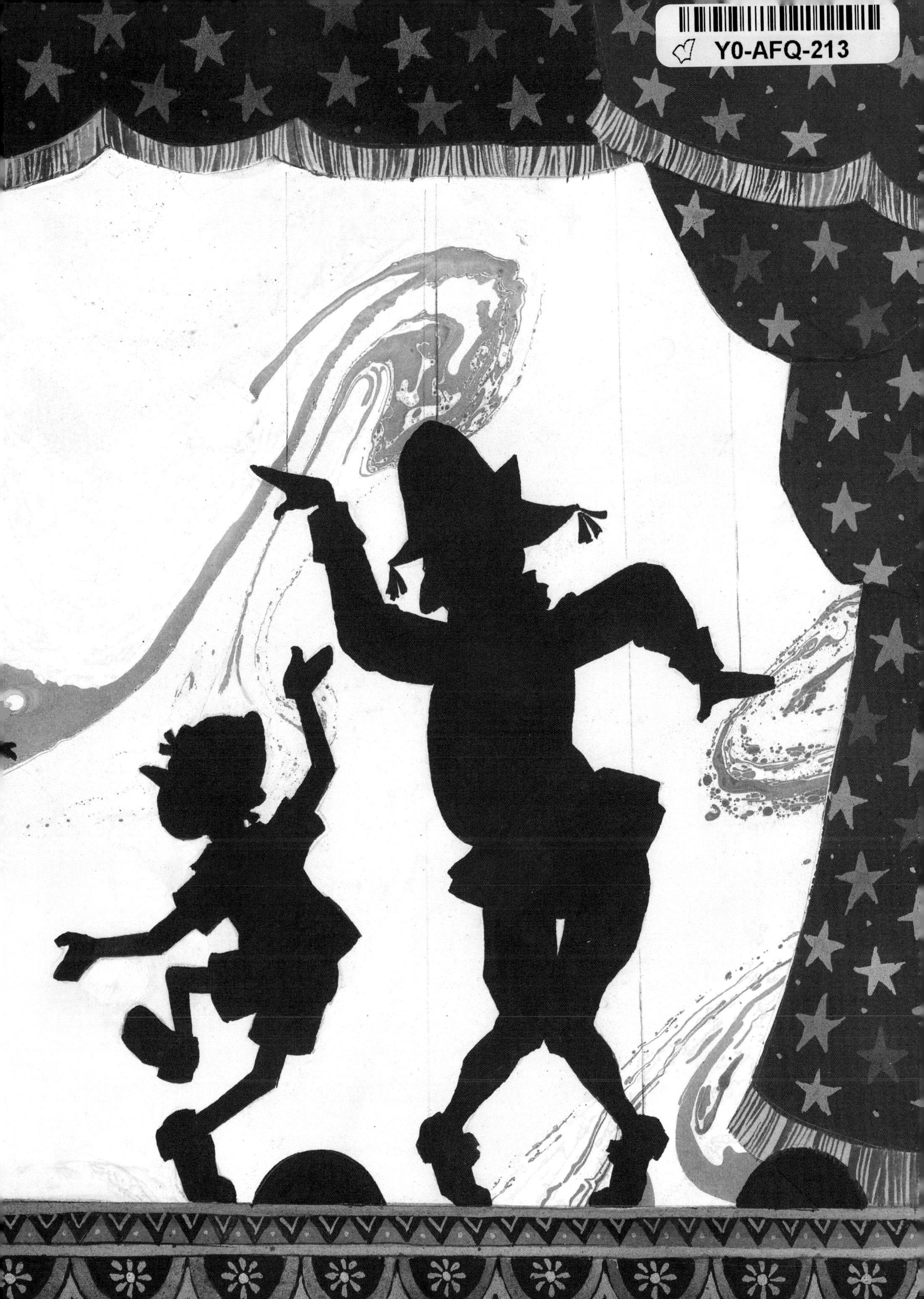

DERRYDALE BOOKS
New York/Avenel, New Jersey
Copyright © 1992 by Peter Haddock Ltd, England
All rights reserved.
This 1992 edition is published by Derrydale Books.
distributed by Outlet Book Company, Inc.,
a Random House Company,
40 Engelhard Avenue
Avenel, New Jersey 07001.

Printed and Bound in Singapore

ISBN: 0-517-08666-2

8 7 6 5 4 3 2 1

Pinocchio

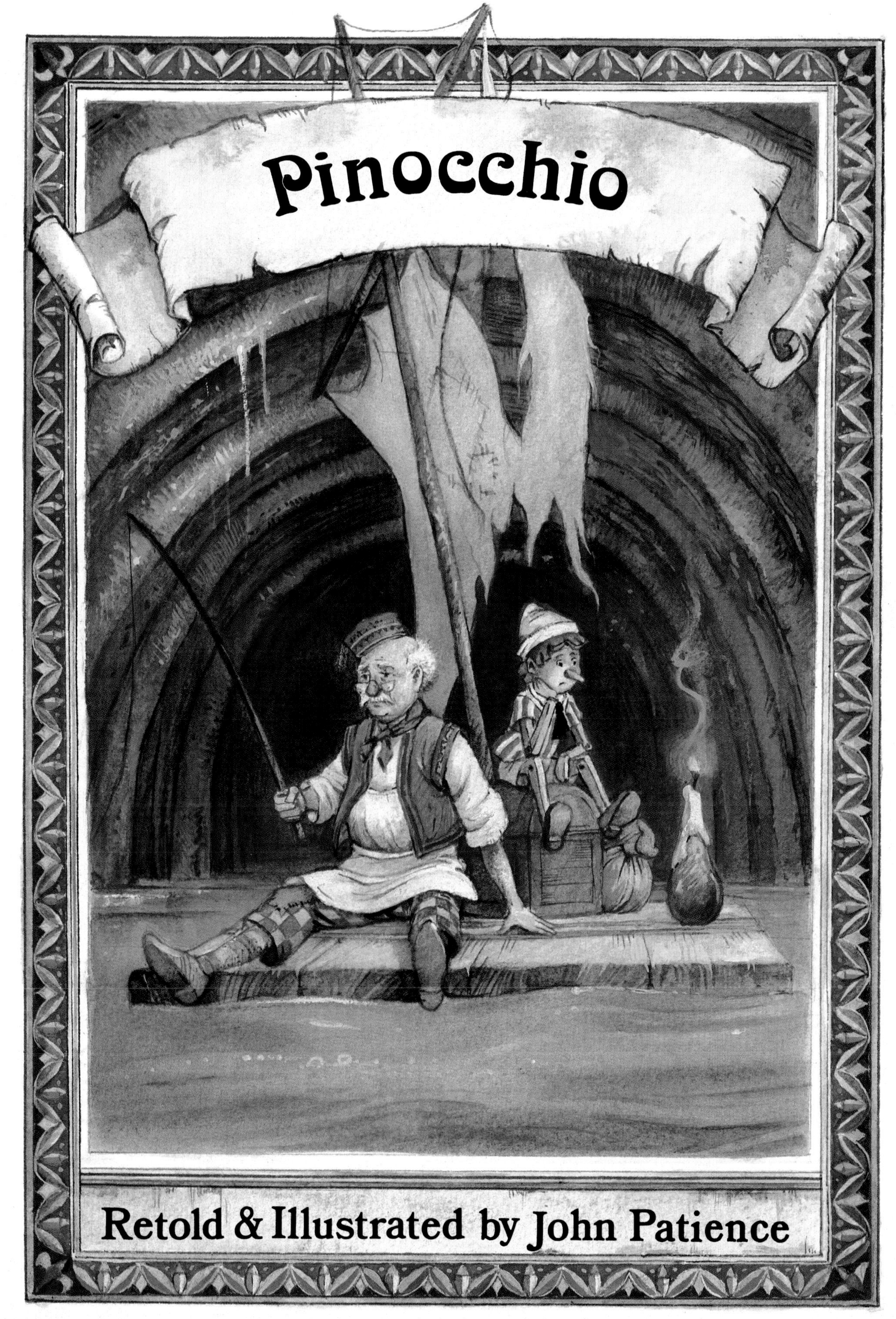

Retold & Illustrated by John Patience

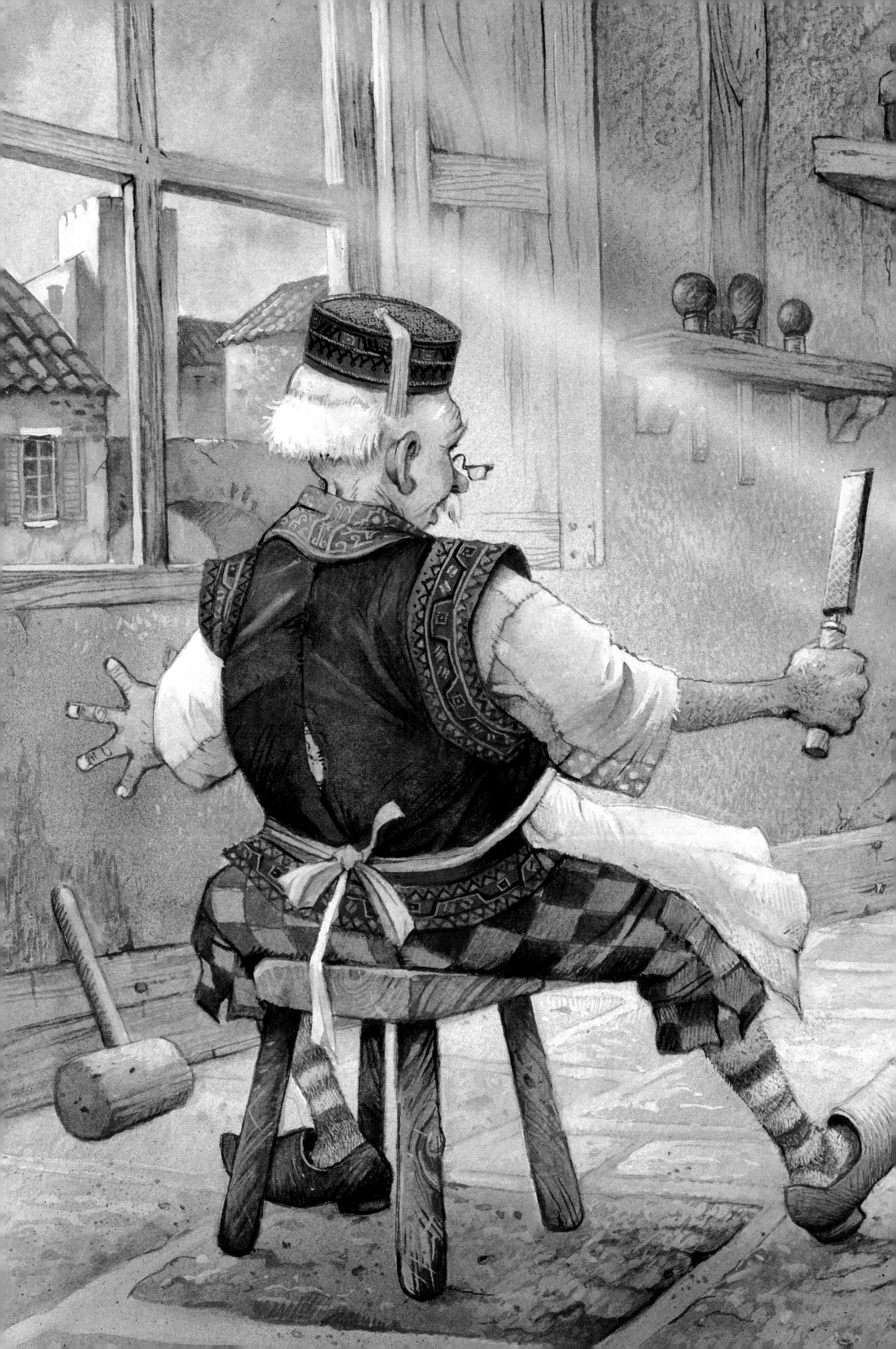

There was once an old wood carver named Geppetto who longed for a son to keep him company. One day Geppetto was carving a puppet. He had just finished making the head when suddenly it winked at him. Geppetto thought he must be imagining things and continued with his work. But as soon as he had finished the puppet's legs it jumped off the old man's lap and began to dance around on the floor. "You are alive, just like a real boy!" gasped Geppetto. "I will call you Pinocchio."

The old man was delighted with the puppet and made him some beautiful clothes. "You must go to school and learn to read and write," said Geppetto. "I'm afraid I can't go," replied Pinocchio. "I have no spelling book."

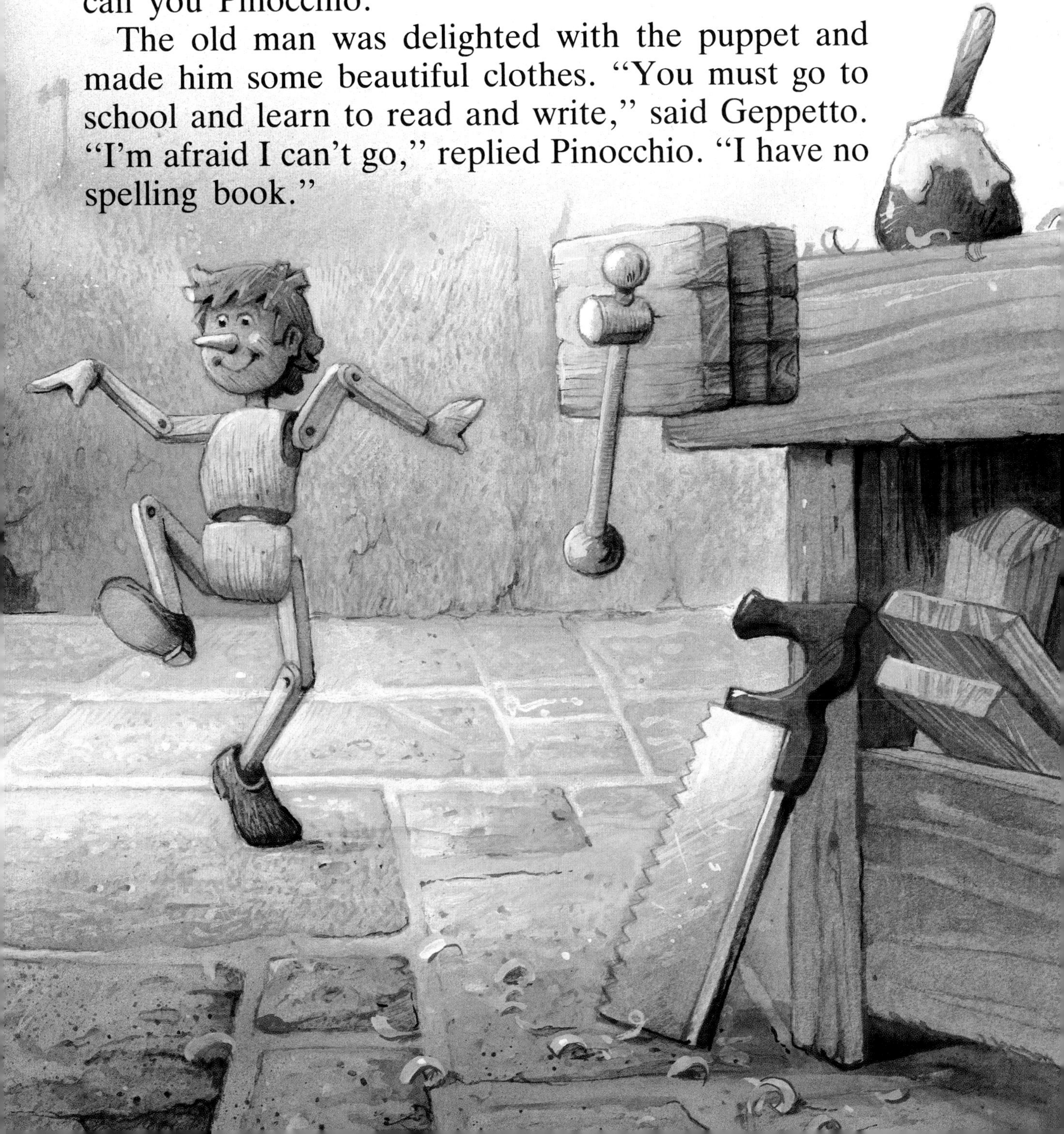

Geppetto was very sad because he had no money, so what did he do but sell his only coat so that he could buy his puppet son a spelling book. The next day Pinocchio set out for school, but on the way he passed a theatre. The ungrateful puppet forgot all about his father's sacrifice. He sold his spelling book to buy a ticket and went inside. Pinocchio was amazed. All the actors were puppets. "Hooray!" he cried. "They are my true brothers." And he jumped up onto the stage.

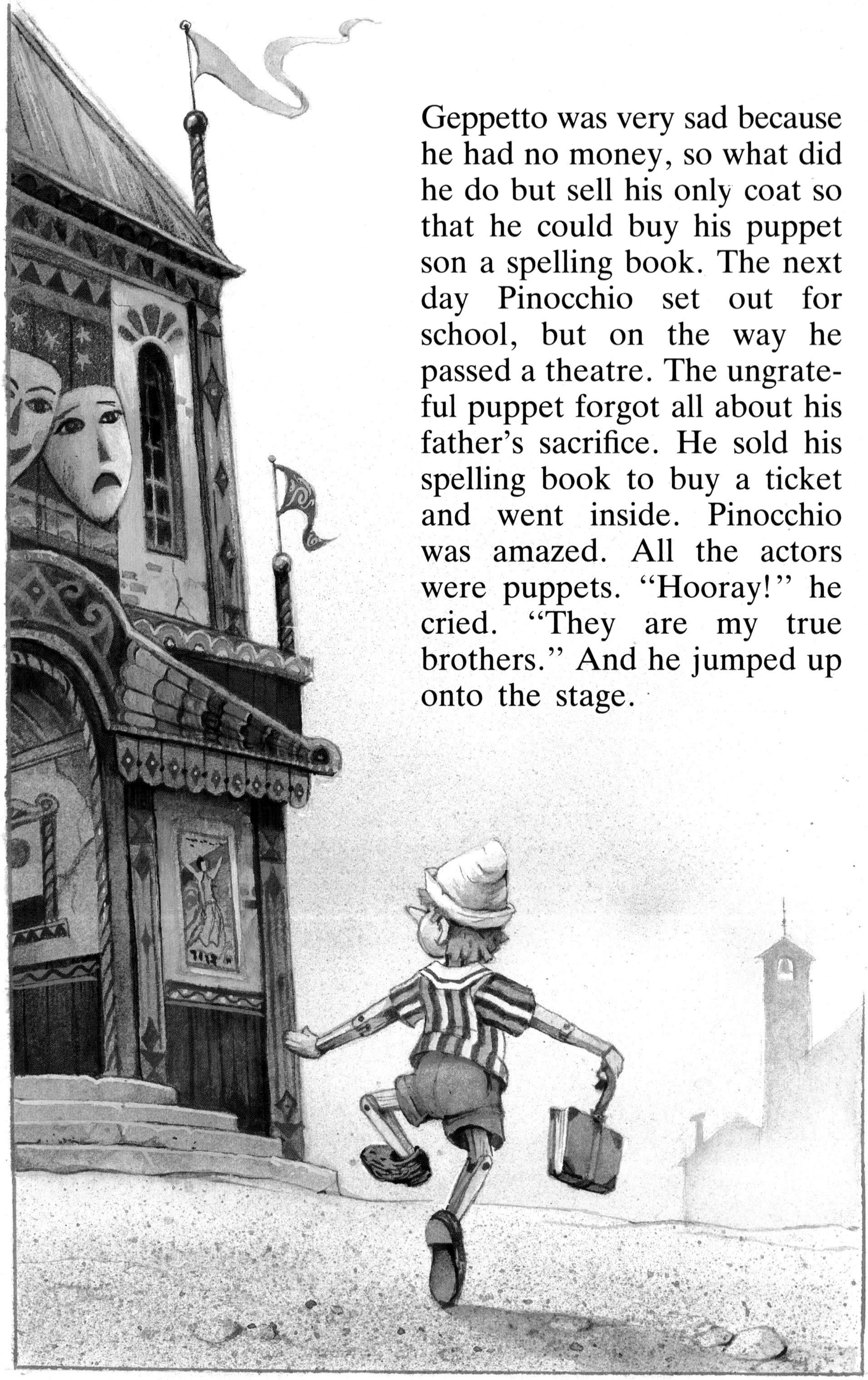

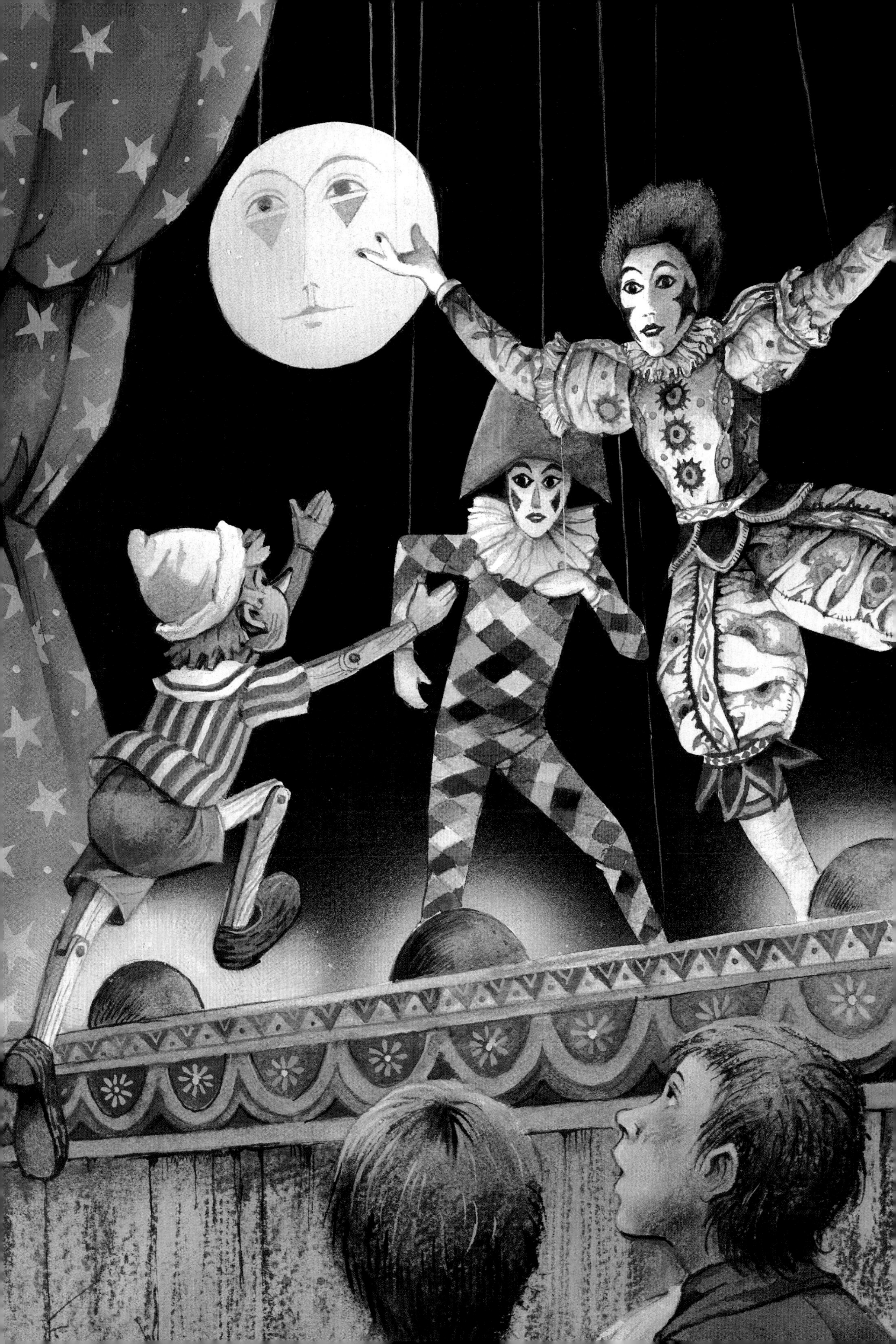

"Boo!" shouted the audience. "You are spoiling the show." But Pinocchio went on dancing with the other puppets. Soon the puppet master came to see what the trouble was. At first he was inclined to chop Pinocchio up and throw him on the fire, but the puppet pleaded so piteously for his life that he changed his mind. "Very well, I shall burn Harlequin instead," he growled. But Pinocchio was brave. "Do not burn Harlequin for he has done no wrong," he cried. "Burn me after all." These brave words touched the puppet master's heart. "I'll go without fire tonight," he exclaimed. "And you shall have a reward for your courage. Take these gold pieces and off you go."

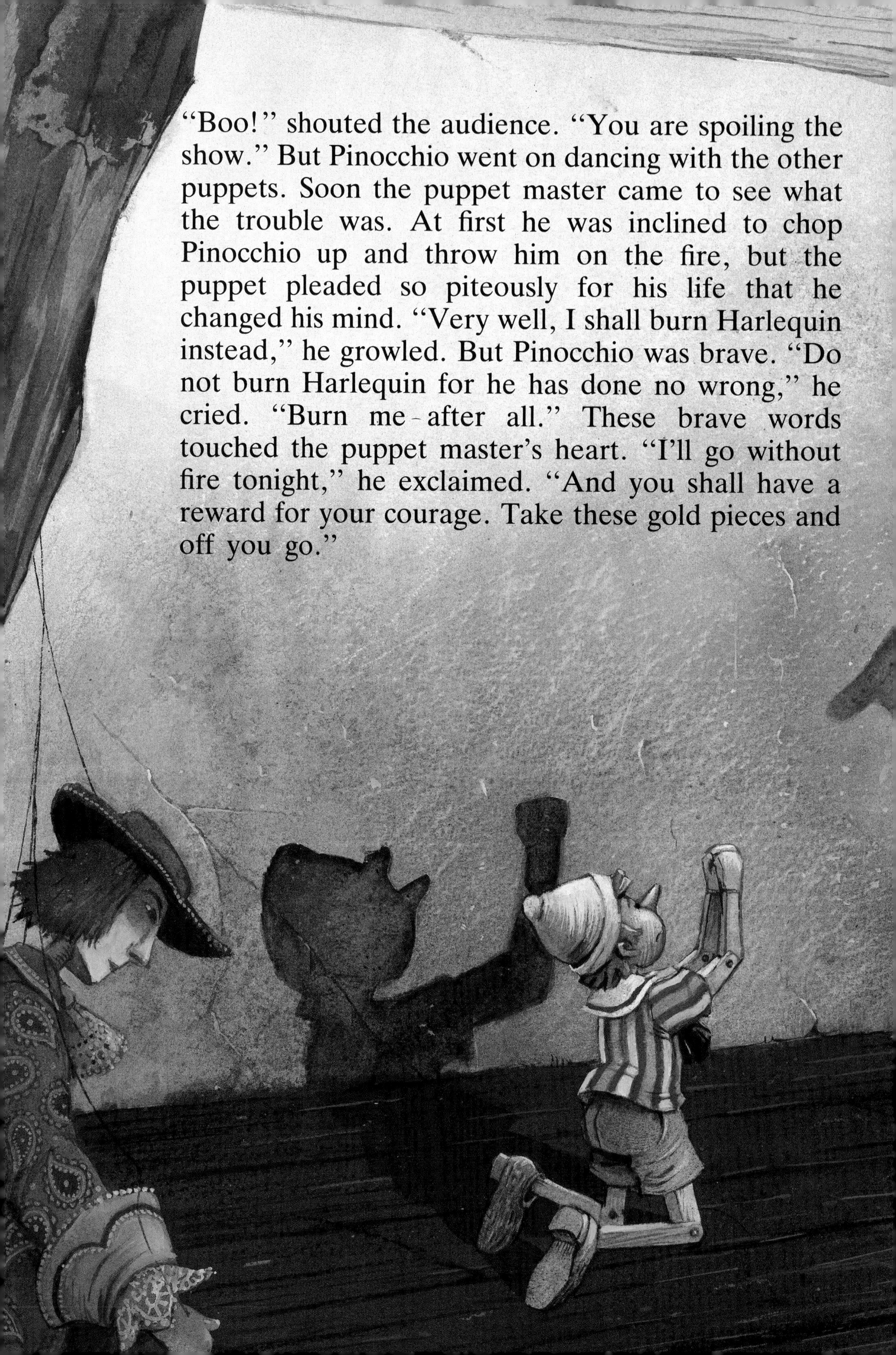

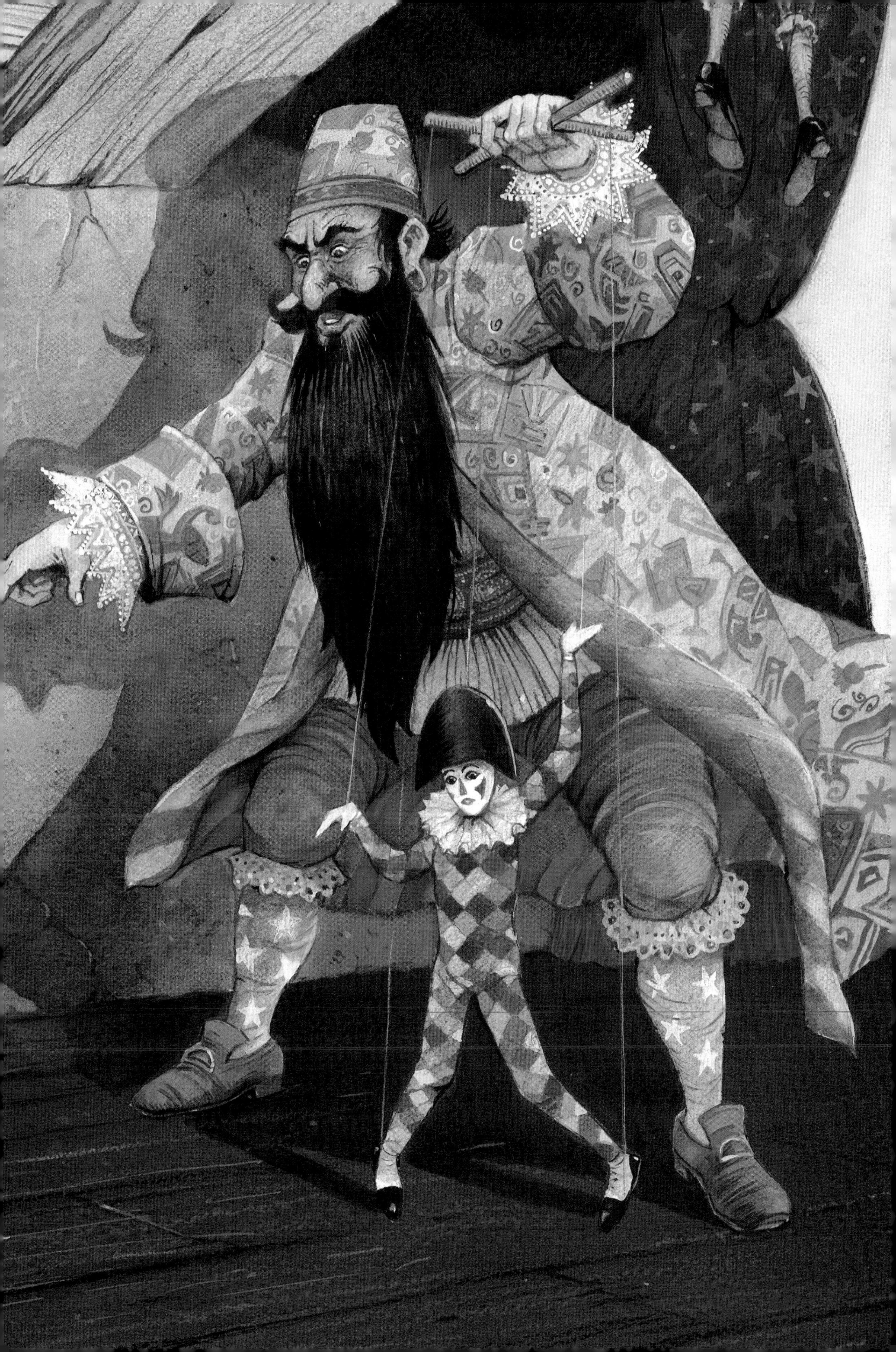

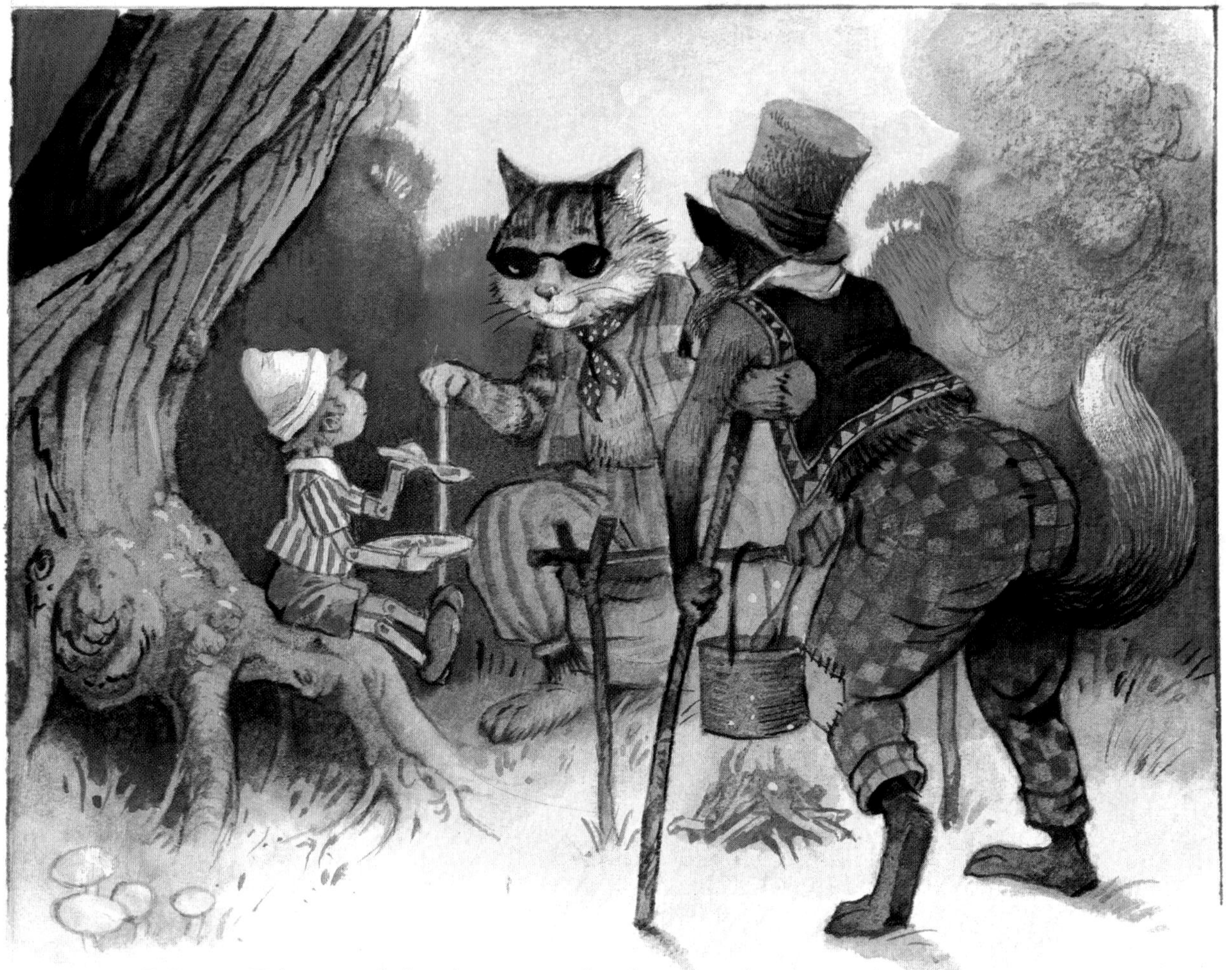

Now Pinocchio honestly intended to buy his father a new coat and himself a new spelling book. However on the way home he met with a fox and a cat. The fox pretended to be lame and the cat pretended to be blind.

In fact the fox and the cat were a couple of rogues. They invited Pinocchio to share their supper. While he ate, the puppet told the villains all about the puppet master and his gold pieces.

Later the cat and the fox said goodbye and went on their way, but they hid themselves in the wood. They put on masks and hoods and as Pinocchio passed by they sprang upon him. Fortunately Pinocchio had time to hide the gold pieces in his mouth. When the fox and the cat failed to find the money they were angry. They tied up the puppet and left him dangling from a tree.

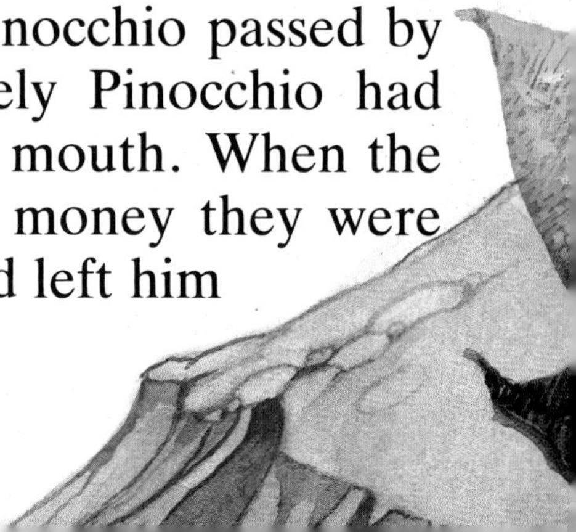

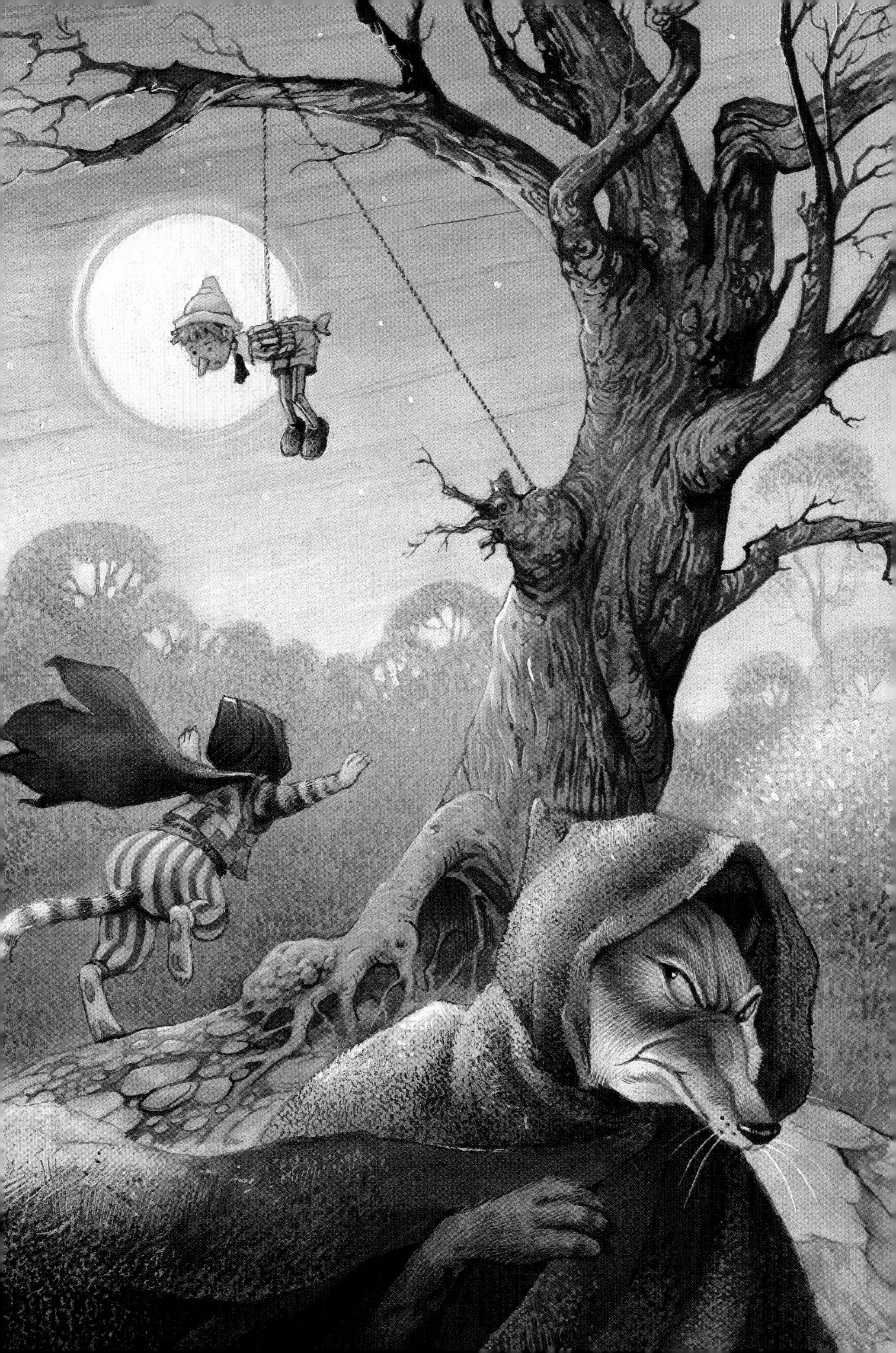

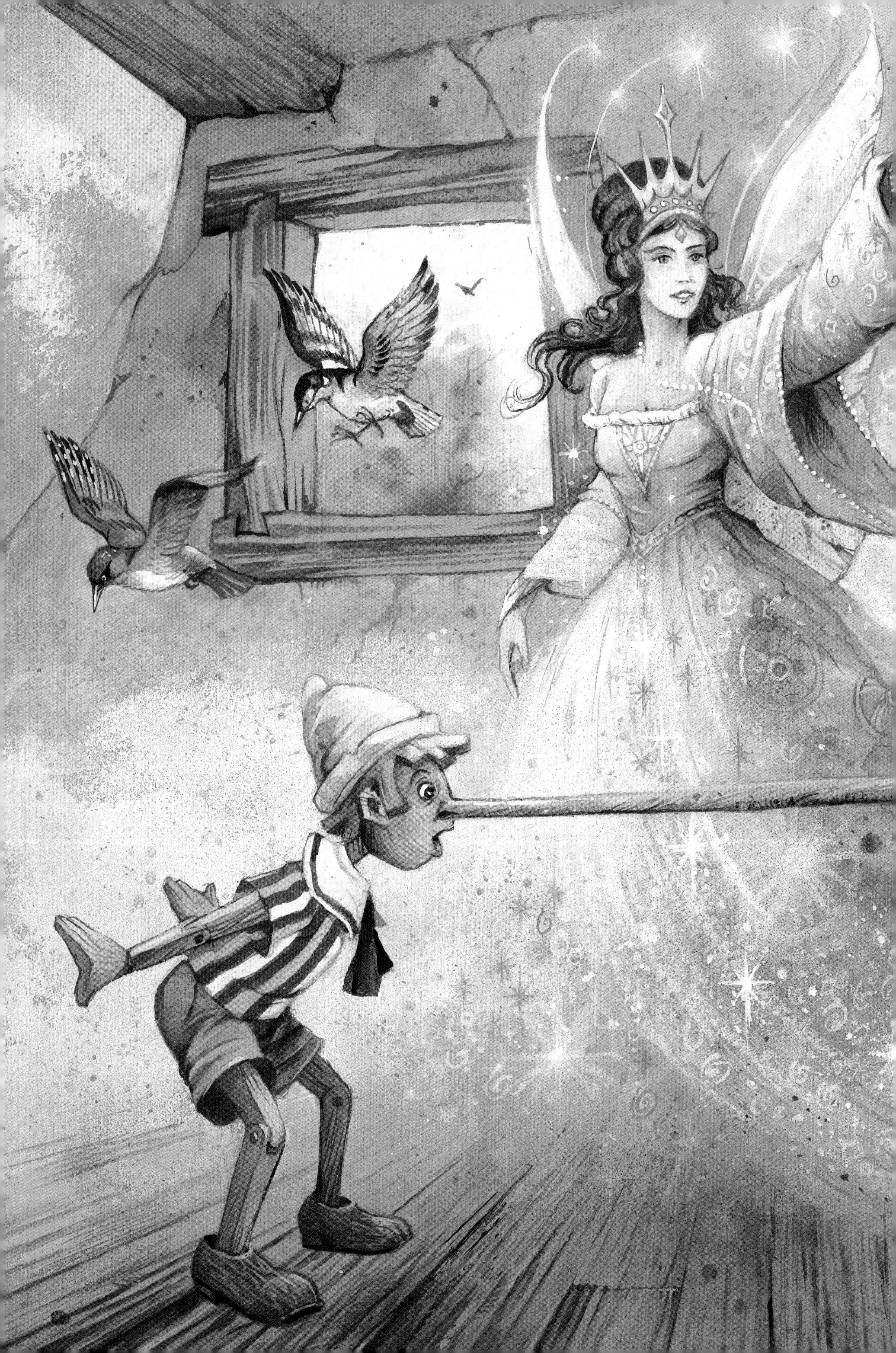

Now the blue fairy who lived in the woods flew to Pinocchio's rescue and took him to her home. "How did this happen?" she asked. Pinocchio began to tell her, but when he came to the part about the gold pieces he told a lie. He said the thieves had stolen them, but they were in his pocket. As soon as he told this lie, Pinocchio's nose grew two inches longer. He told another lie and his nose grew longer still and it went on growing until at last he could not get it through the door.

Then the blue fairy took pity on him. She called for some woodpeckers. They flew in through the window and pecked Pinocchio's nose back to its right length.

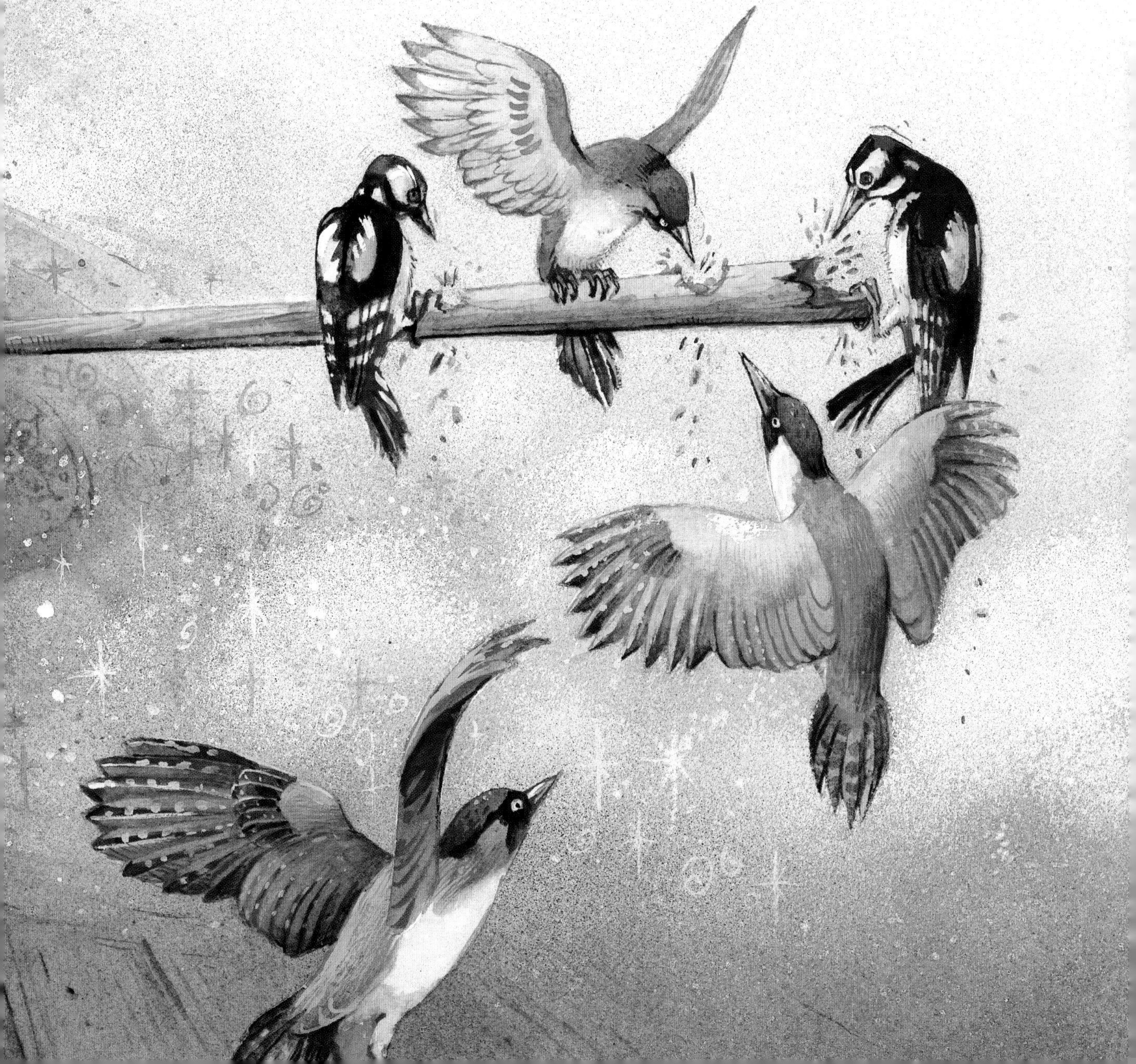

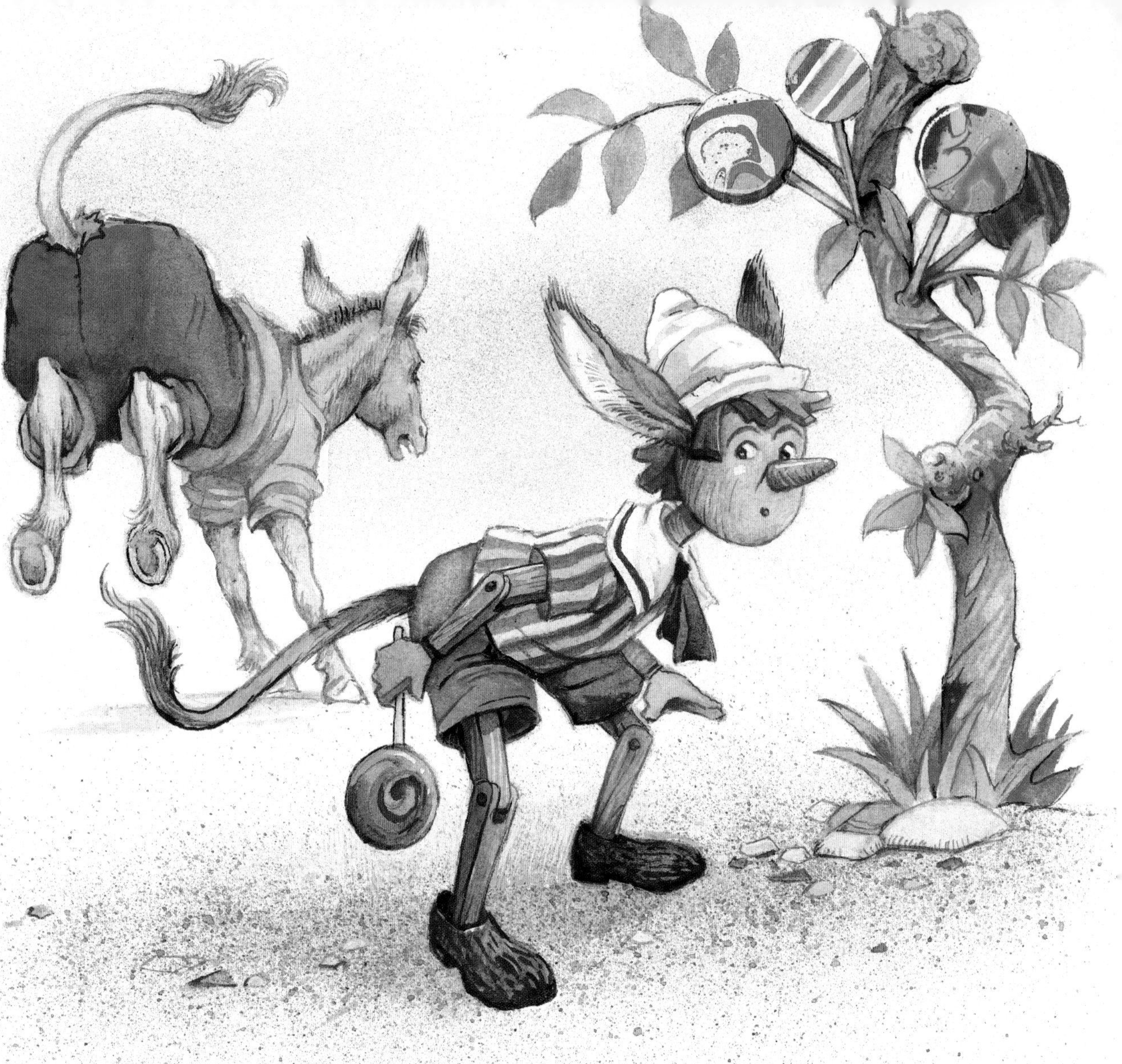

Pinocchio had learned his lesson. He promised never to tell another lie. He thanked the blue fairy for helping him and said goodbye. He knew that he ought to make his way back to his father. Instead he listened to a naughty boy who told him, "I know a place called Toyland where there is no school to go to, no rules to keep and lollipops grow on trees!"

At first Pinocchio had a wonderful time in Toyland. It was fun and games from morning till night. But all fun and no work was very bad for Pinocchio. He grew long, furry ears, a tail and hooves and he changed into a DONKEY! The wizard who ruled over Toyland sold Pinocchio to a circus and he was made to perform tricks to amuse the crowd.

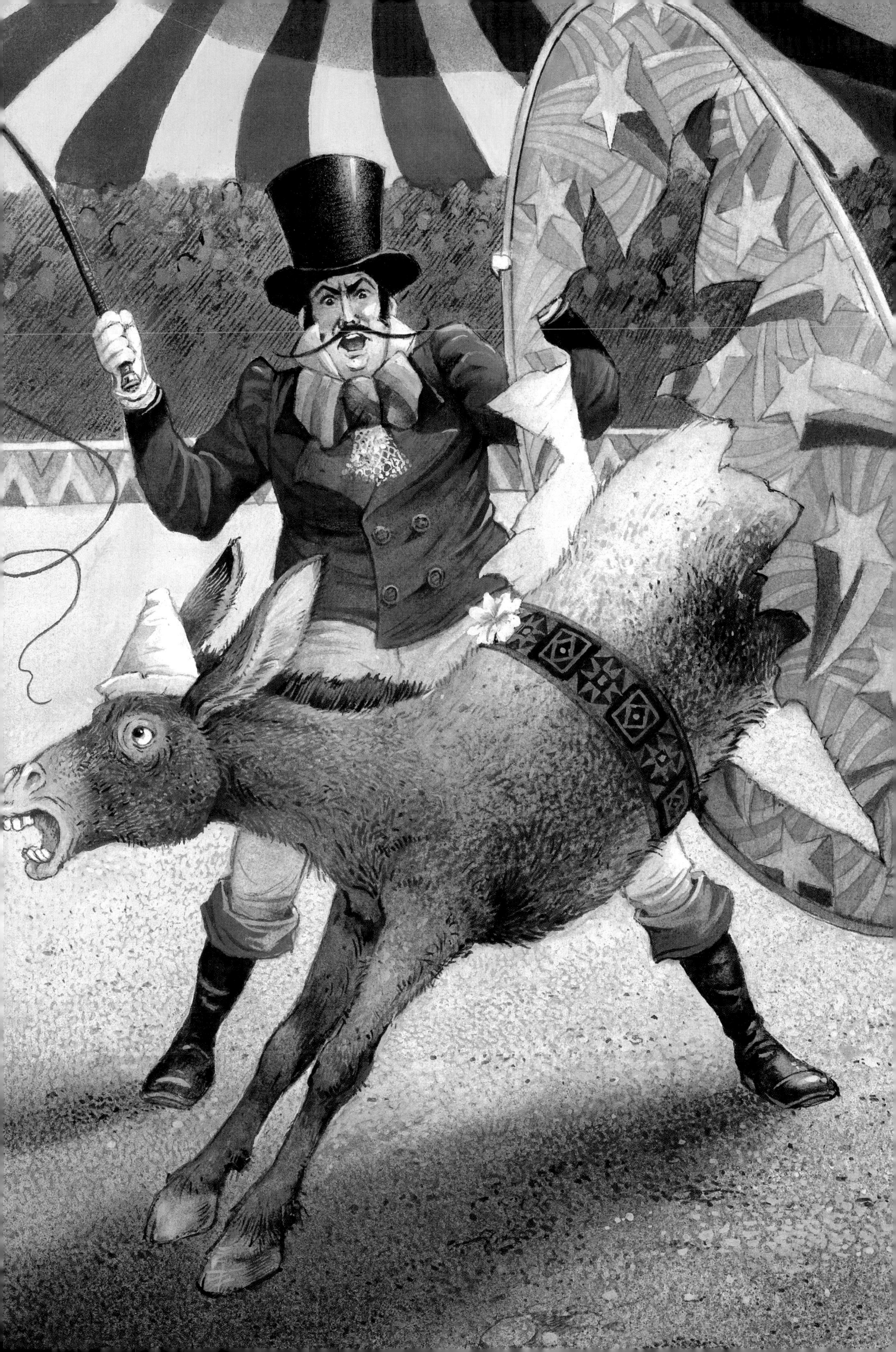

One day, when Pinocchio was forced to jump through a big hoop, he stumbled and fell. This made him lame. He was no use to the circus now. The cruel ringmaster took him to a cliff and threw him down into the sea.

As soon as he was cast into the water the spell was broken and Pinocchio was changed back into a puppet. Alas, he was instantly swallowed up by a monstrous fish. Miraculously it was the same fish that had swallowed his father Geppetto when he had sailed out to search for Pinocchio. "My poor son!" cried Geppetto, hugging the puppet. "Now you too are a prisoner in this terrible place!"

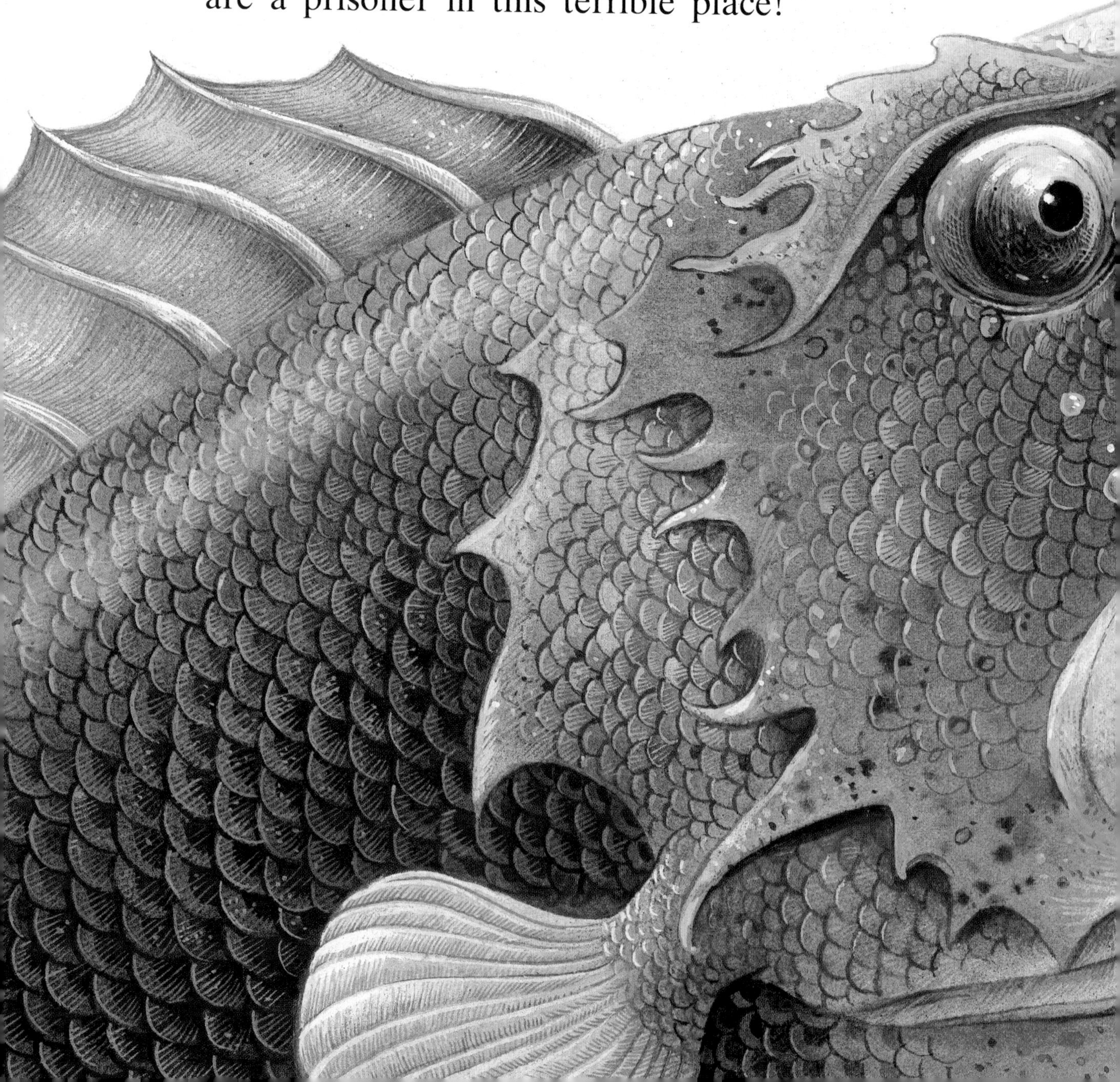

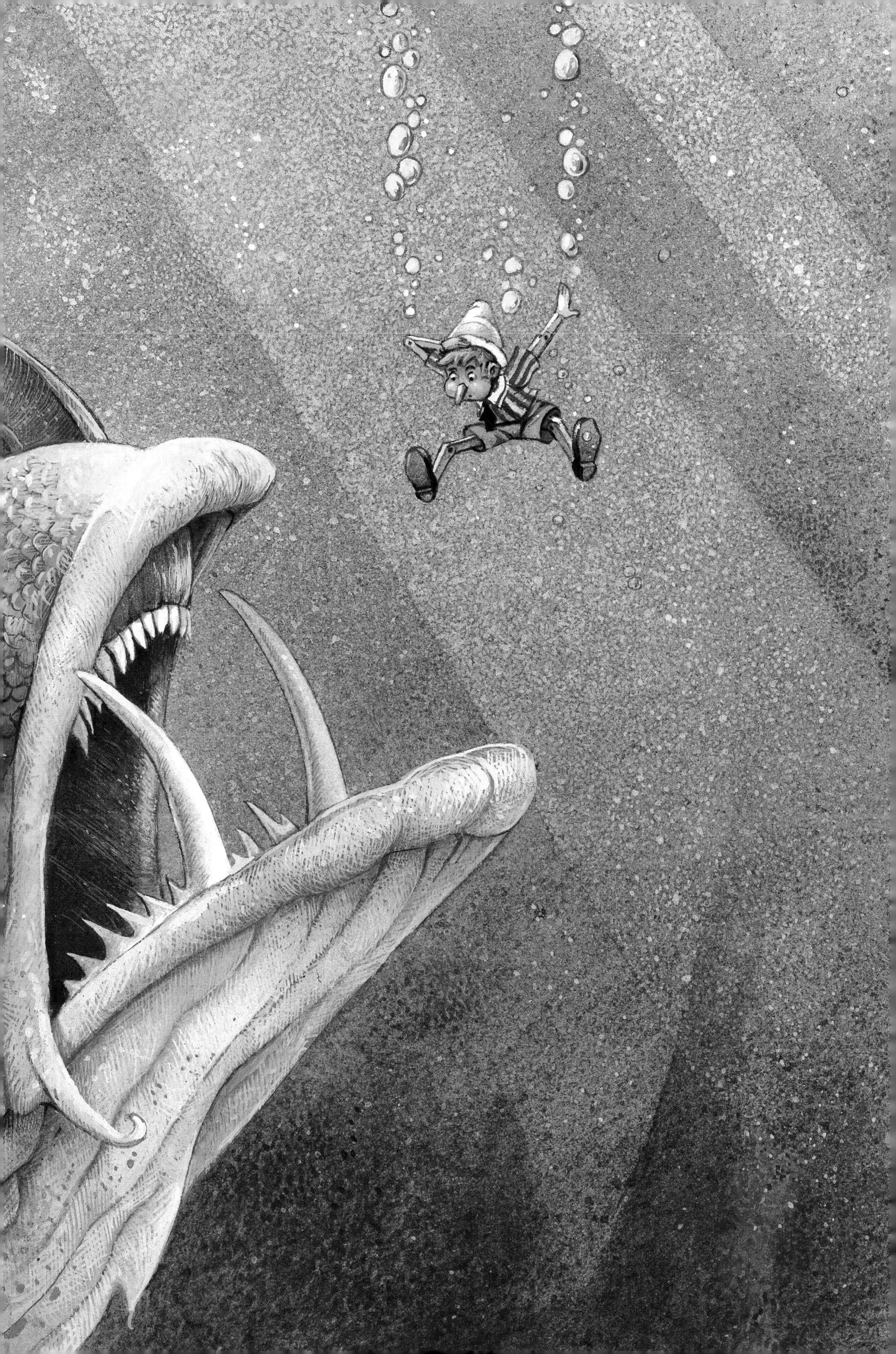

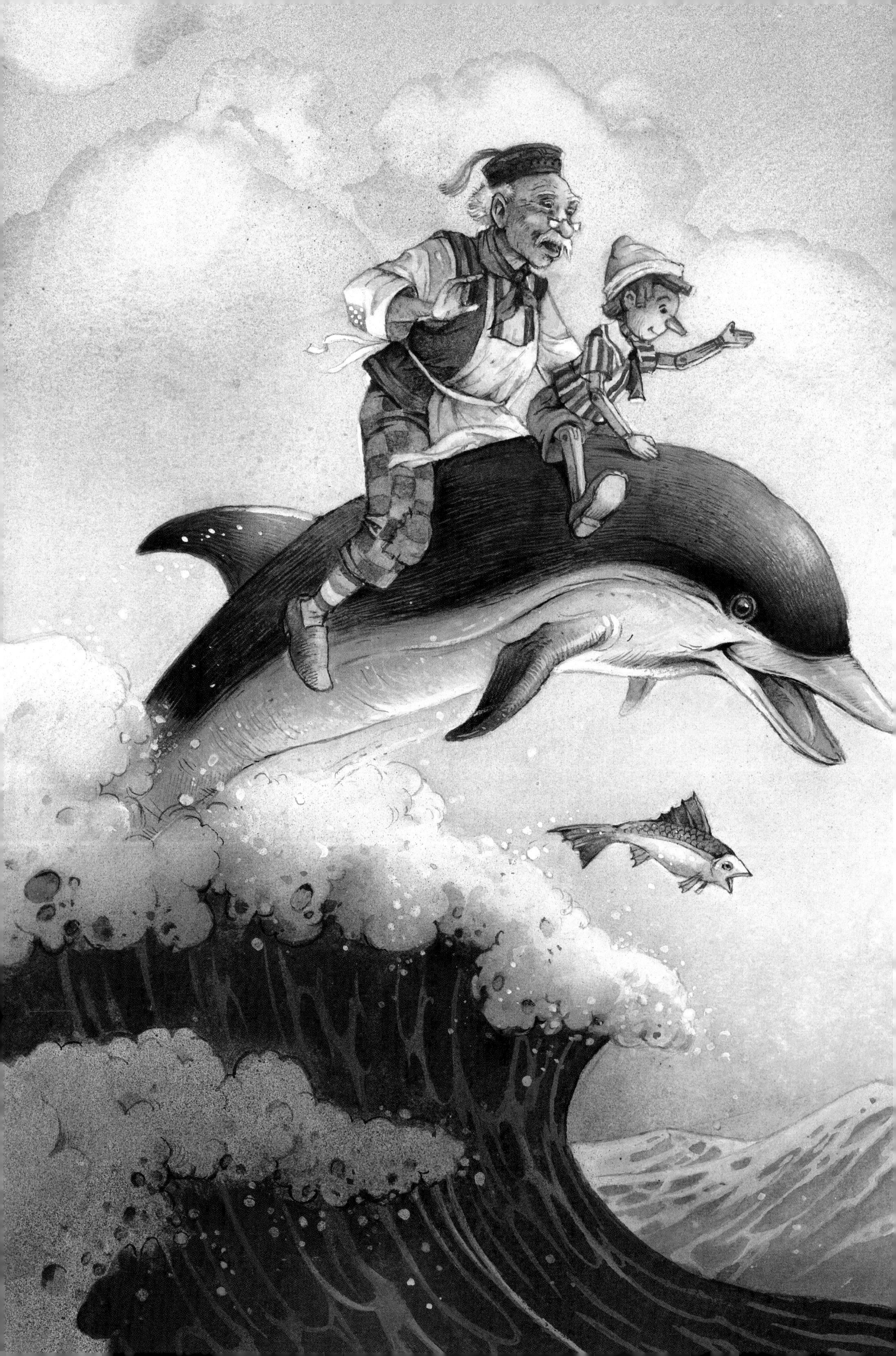

Pinocchio and Geppetto lived inside the giant fish for a long, long time. Then one day, quite suddenly, the monster gave a great sneeze. The wood carver and the puppet found themselves shooting forward, out through the fish's open mouth. They swam up to the surface of the sea. There they found a friendly dolphin who carried them both safely back to shore.

"I will never leave you again, Father," promised Pinocchio when they were home. As he spoke a strange light began to shimmer around the puppet and he was transformed into a real boy! It was the work of the blue fairy who had rewarded Pinocchio for his courage.

Geppetto was overjoyed. His dearest wish had come true!

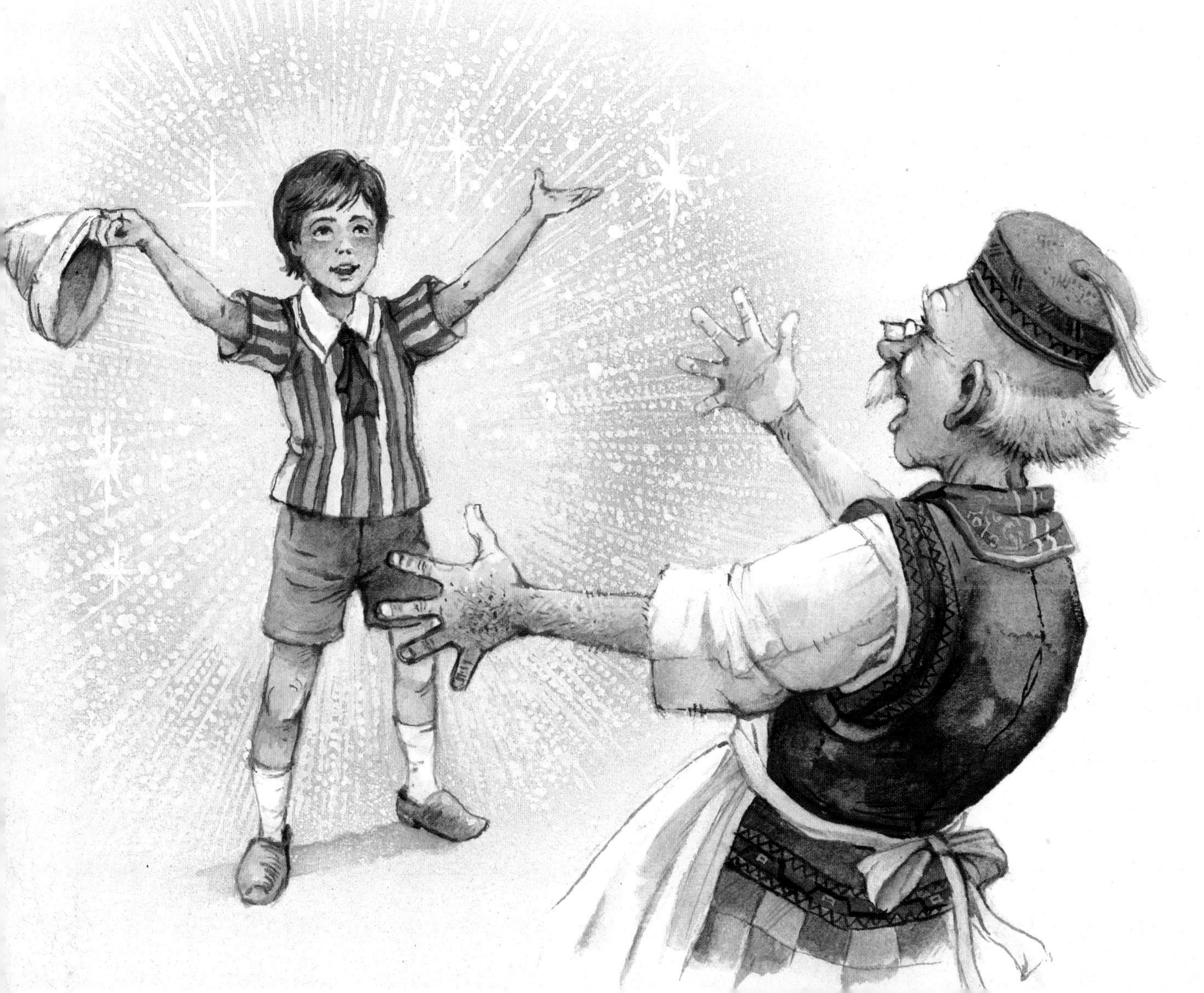

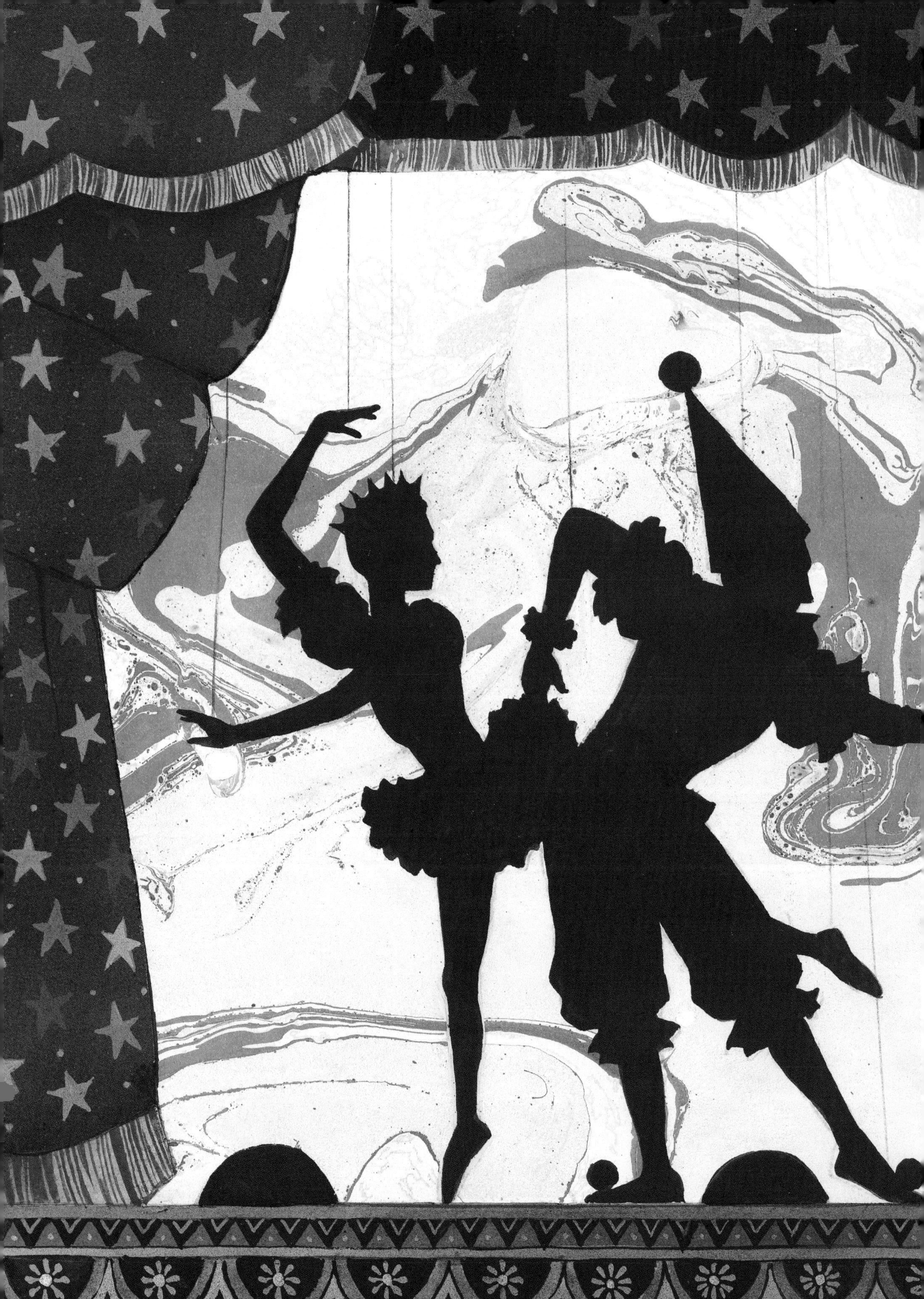